The Mud Fairy

Amy Young

BLOOMSBURY

NEW YORK BERLIN LONDON

To Zoe, the original mud fairy

Published by Bloomsbury U.S.A. Children's Books
175 Fifth Avenue, New York, New York 10010

Library of Congress Cataloging-in-Publication Data
Young, Amy.
The Mud Fairy / by Amy Young. — 1st U.S. ed.
p.   cm.
Summary: Emmalina the fairy describes how, after many efforts, she finally earned her wings.
ISBN 978-1-59990-104-6 (hardcover) • ISBN 978-1-59990-312-5 (reinforced)
[1. Fairies—Fiction. 2. Frogs—Fiction.] I. Title.
PZ7.Y845Mu 2010   [E]—dc22   2009018252

Art created using gouache on Fabriano Uno soft press watercolor paper
Typeset in Georgia
Book design by Danielle Delaney

First U.S. Edition March 2010
Printed in China by Printplus Limited, Shenzhen, Guangdong
2 4 6 8 10 9 7 5 3 1 (hardcover)
2 4 6 8 10 9 7 5 3 1 (reinforced)

Oh, you may think that being a fairy is all fun and easy, and that we just flit around from flower to flower and play games. Ha! My name is Emmalina, and I'm here to tell you that fairy life is not all that it's cracked up to be.

A fairy is supposed to be neat and dainty all the time—no running, no jumping, no playing in the mud. She is supposed to sit up straight, sip dewdrops, and nibble pollen pie—no slurping, no gulping, no burping.

Me, I'd rather play in the
swamp with the frogs.
I usually get into trouble.

The hardest part about being a fairy? When a fairy gets to be one hundred years old, like me, she has to *earn* her wings. She has to be good at something important.

Leapfrog is not considered important.

Twink opened a flower.
She got *her* wings.

I tried to open a flower,

but it didn't work out very well.

Sparkletoes strung dewdrops
on a spiderweb.

She got *her* wings.

I tried to do the
same thing, but
the situation
got sticky.

Corabelle, Delilah, Fern, Skye, and
Indigo teamed up to make a rainbow.
It was beautiful! Of course they all got
their wings.

But when I tried to do something fancy?
You guessed it—no one appreciated it.

"Maybe you are trying too hard, Emmalina," said the queen. "Every fairy is good at something. Just give it a little time."

What if I wasn't good at *anything*?

I snuck off to the swamp. My frog friends
were sitting around wringing their feet.
"Oh, Emmalina!" they croaked.
"Something is wrong with our children!"

"Look!" said Garrump. "Junior can't jump.
He can't catch flies! None of them can!"

Well, you don't get to be as old as I am without learning a thing or two.

"They're tadpoles," I said. "They'll turn into frogs. Just give them a little time."

I came back every day to see
how the tadpoles were doing.

One day I
chased away a
hungry monster.

Another day I hid
them from a giant.

As the weeks went by, the tadpoles
got little nubs on their bodies, which
slowly turned into arms and legs.

Finally, one day all of the tadpoles had turned into frogs. "Look, look!" cheered their parents. "They will be jumpers yet! *Ribbit–ribbit–HOORAY!*"

I spent the rest of the day teaching the new
frogs how to play leapfrog and catch flies.

When I got home, the queen was waiting for me.

"Emmalina," she said, "I know what you have been doing."

Uh-oh. I was in big trouble now. I was muddy and messy, not dainty and delicate at all. I even smelled kind of froggy.

But then the queen smiled. "You helped the frogs
with their tadpoles, and you taught the new frogs how
to leap and play. No other fairy could have done that.

You have earned your wings, with high honors.
You will henceforth be known as Emmalina the
Mud Fairy, Protector of Frogs."

We celebrated with the biggest party you have ever seen. Fairies got muddy and frogs got flowery. We danced and played until dawn.

Sure, some fairies flit around from flower to flower all day.

Me, I love being the Mud Fairy.